THREE PIRATES and YOU!

Written by Lisa Vischer

Illustrated by Tom Bancroft

BIG IDEA
BOOKS®

Zonderkidz

Zonderkidz.

The children's group of Zondervan

www.zonderkidz.com

Three Pirates and You!
ISBN: 0-310-70724-2
Copyright © 2004 by Big Idea Productions, Inc.
Illustrations copyright © 2004 by Big Idea Productions, Inc.

Requests for information should be addressed to:
Zonderkidz, Grand Rapids, Michigan 49530

Editor: Cindy Kenney
Art Direction and Design: Karen Poth

Printed in China
04 05 06 07/HK/4 3 2 1

There once were three pirates who all the day long
just sat doing nothing but singing their song.

These pirates were lazy, as lazy could be.
Their only adventure was watching TV.

"I'm tired!" said Larry, "Of being so bored."
"I'd have to agree," said the decorative gourd.

"Me too!" said Pa Grape, "We need something to do!
But I can't think of what. And I don't know with who!"

Then all of a sudden, they all noticed **YOU!**

"Hey, look over there!
Do you see what I see?
There seems to be
somebody looking at me!"

"Don't panic, now Larry. It's only a book.

These things sometimes happen. We'll give it a look."

"GREAT SCOTT!

You weren't kidding! Oh, joy! Can it be?
We've waited two years and a month patiently
for this special moment to find a new friend!
Our days of frustration have come to an end."

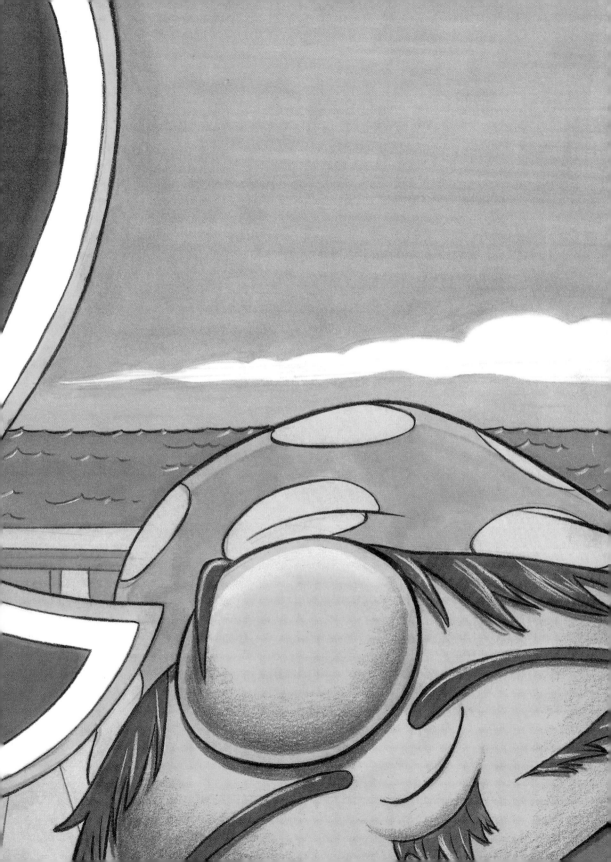

"We want an adventure! We're no longer tired.
In fact, thanks to you, we are feeling inspired!"
So come on along for a journey or two.
We'll make lots of plans for three pirates and **YOU!**
We suddenly have an idea or two.

WE COULD . . .

... Sail away to Greenland!
We could take a trip to Denver!
We could have our lunch in Lombard
at a food court in the mall!

We could sail around Alaska,

take a trip to see Nebraska,

and be sure to visit Boston in the fall!

WE COULD . . .

...find some mashed potatoes
on vacation in Barbados
just to see if they'd enjoy
a close encounter with a wall.

Kiss a chipmunk, pluck a rooster,
play some ping-pong at a shoe store
and buy tickets to see
Boston in the fall!

WE COULD . . .

...wear a red bandana,
ride a bike to Texarkana,
after painting yellow daisies
on a big red rubber ball.

Then we'll sniff the little stinkbug
that lives under Larry's bathtub
that was shipped to him
from Boston in the fall!

WE COULD . . .

...finally visit Tampa,
say hello to Larry's Grandpa,
or go bury all our treasure
in St. Louis or St. Paul.

BUT...

Of all the things that we could do,

The main thing we should *really* do

IS FINALLY VISIT BOSTON IN THE FALL!

"Sounds good!" said Pa Grape,
"But my friends, I have found,
I'm tired already! I need to lie down!"

"Me too!" said the others,
who looked somewhat dizzy.
"It's been quite a day.
We've been terribly busy!"

"It's true, we've been lazy
but those days are numbered.
Because of YOUR help
now we feel unencumbered!"

"Because YOU'RE our friend now,
we've never felt finer.
But now we must sit,
and enjoy our recliner."

"Before we doze off,
one more thing that's so true:
we're thankful that God gave us
friends just like **YOU!**"